COLD WOODS

A Splatterpunk Novella

Jerry Blaze

Unveiling Nightmares Press

Dedicated to Paige Ray
Thanks for everything!

ONE

The cabin was lit with a crisp fire in the fireplace and black smoke danced as it rose from the chimney, it was an ideal vacation getaway.

The nights were cold on the mountain. Even during the summer the air was frigid and frost touched the leaves in early morning sunshine.

Martin Brockton was here at the cabin to spend a night or two away from the hustle and bustle of big city life. His divorce was nearly finalized and his kids were hellbent on making sure he suffered for their mother leaving him, so it was nice to get away. All he needed was a cup of hot coffee, a blanket and a good book.

He was a short and thin man, with a head of red hair, while his face was covered in freckles that didn't fade with age. Life as an insurance agent had also proved to be one of the worst decisions of his adult life.

Still, he could enjoy the little things, including the crackle of embers in the dancing fires that lit up the inside of the cabin. He didn't mind it. The sound of howling outside was one of the things that kept him up at night when he tried to sleep, yet this time there were few howls and even fewer nature sounds to disturb him.

For now, he was just going to watch the fires dance and pour a mug of fresh black coffee.

Sitting on the couch with his cup, he picked up the book that was laying on the coffee table in front of the couch and flipped open to the page he'd bookmarked it. The book was a bit of historical fiction about Jack the Ripper going to the Old West. It was a fun little read that he was enjoying with each passing chapter.

The warmth of the fireplace added an extra layer to the comfort he felt whilst reading his book. It was a great way to destress after his life had been upended by his bitch ex-wife. She had the balls to say he wasn't paying enough attention to her and yet, he was working full-time shifts just to make ends meet while she did nothing. Their kids were in their teens and focusing on whatever kids are into now, they never fucking told him a thing about their lives.

Not that it mattered, he didn't care in the least, they were making him the bad guy in this whole situation and he didn't have time for that kind of negativity.

The sky outside had grown dark with clouds and Martin was ready for a late night. He didn't have anything else planned beyond finishing his book and catching a bit of shut-eye before taking on the next book. Reading was all he could enjoy anymore. Nothing else about life seemed remotely interesting.

He was probably on the verge of a nervous breakdown or, at the very least, a diagnosis of clinical depression. His whole life had been spent on making his family happy and now, when he needed them the most, they had abandoned him. His elderly mother in the home couldn't be bothered to talk to him and his father had died years earlier, so it wasn't like he had his own parents to turn to.

Being an only child was one of the worst parts of it all.

Plus, to add insult to injury, his best friend had since revealed he was seeing Martin's soon-to-be-ex-wife and couldn't even be bothered to listen to reason. It was a nightmare. Life was turning into a straight up nightmare.

Enough, he thought to himself, he needed to focus on the book and try to enjoy what the storyline had for him. Thankfully it was a fast-paced plot and had plenty of action for him to pay attention to while he sipped his coffee.

A knock at the door caught his attention and he raised up from the couch, setting the book down. Martin walked over to the door and spoke into it, "Can I help you?"

Nobody answered.

He spoke a bit louder, "Hello?"

A brisk, feminine voice responded, "Please, you must help me, they are coming."

"Who?"

"Them. The mountain folk."

Martin considered what she said. Mountain folk? There wasn't anyone on the mountains in all the years he'd been coming to the cabin. It was a barren area. He opened the door slightly, looking out to the person on the porch, "Who?"

The person was a petite woman with short hair that had been cut with jagged precision and caked-on dirt covered her pale skin, her body bundled up in a blanket made of bearskin though it seemed that's all that she wore. She whispered, "Please, may I come in?"

"Sure, you must be freezing," Martin opened the door wider and let the young girl enter the cabin, watching as she sat on the couch. He closed the door and turned to her, "What's your name?"

"Runa. Please, you have to get us out of here, they are coming and they won't hesitate to kill anyone they find on their land," the girl shuddered, her bare arms held the bearskin tighter around her naked frame. Martin swallowed, looking around the cabin for any potential weapons, though he was still not entirely sure he believed her. Kids always get weird notions when they hallucinate on acid or weed or whatever. He offered her his cup of coffee, "Drink this, it'll warm you up."

"There's no time," she replied, drinking quickly, "We have to leave, now, soon!"

"Miss, I can assure you, there's nobody out there."

"You don't know that. I promise you. They are coming."

The sound of a thump came from outside the door and Martin looked over to see her duck her head in the bearskin, "They are here."

Martin hesitated before turning to open the door and look into the darkness on the porch, a shiver hitting him from the blistering winds abounding outside the cabin. The mountain was so cold. The woods surrounding it were bleak and biting, it was a nightmare place to be out with little clothing. The poor girl must have been hallucinating from the cold temperatures.

Turning around to face her from the doorway, Martin shook his head, "Nobody's out here. If you want, I'll take you to town in the morning and we can get help."

No sooner had the words left his lips did the blade of an axe dig into his right shoulder and force him to scream out in terror, falling to the floor of the cabin. He turned, holding his bloody wound, looking up at the person who had struck him and saw four large shadows approaching from the porch. He held his hands up, "Wait!"

The axe swung again and tore his left hand off at the wrist, provoking a heavy cry from him as he held the bleeding stump against his chest. Martin attempted to push himself away by kicking at the floor. Suddenly, the girl dropped her bearskin and her naked body moved behind him, crouching down and taking his arms to keep him from moving away. She giggled,

"Should have taken my warning, city man."

The large man with the axe raised the weapon up and brought it down, splitting the front of Martin's head in half. Martin's face split open, his brains and blood flooded forward all over his body and the floor. The large man looked at the others, their forms entering to drag Martin's corpse out of the cabin whilst the girl stood up.

Her young and lithe form was illuminated by the flickering fireplace. Her breasts were small, her legs were long and her skin covered in goosebumps from the cold air blowing from the open door. She smiled up at the large man who motioned for her to exit the cabin with him; she did as directed, grabbing the bearskin to wrap herself in before departing.

The cabin was a great getaway.

Especially for permanent vacations.

TWO

Lenore Stone gripped the steering wheel of the van tightly; her patience was wearing thin as the load of kids in the car were testing her in every way and there was nobody else there to try to shut them up.

In the seat next to her, her son David was busy arguing and retorting to his sister's boyfriend, Kurt, about the difference between some off the wall subjects. It was an endless argument that the two had. David didn't like Kurt and Kurt didn't like David, it was a constant fight between the two. In the backseat, Carissa had her earphones in and was trying to drown out the noise of the argument between her boyfriend and her brother.

Next to her, her brother's best friend, Kevin, was taking shots at Kurt when David wasn't getting his word. The whole subject was on the idea of a creature in Loch Ness in Scotland and truthfully, it was a stupid subject to argue about. Kurt liked to pick at David and David was hellbent on proving Kurt wrong each time, even if the argument was incapable of being ended peacefully.

Finally, Lenore slammed her fist on the steering wheel, "Everyone shut the fuck up!"

David immediately ceased talking and Kurt did the same, Lenore growled, "David, you're right. Kurt, you're also right. Kevin, you're also right. Carissa, you're right, too."

Carissa looked up, "I didn't say anything?"

"Well, you're right," Lenore huffed, "There, everyone's right, please just shut up."

"Sorry, mum," David whispered, turning to look out the window at the line of trees that were next to the road. It was never like this before. Everything was different now. It was more stress and less joy, he didn't like it, but there was nothing he could do.

His mom was at her wit's end with the

constant arguing and he knew he was wrong, he just hated letting Carissa's boyfriend get the last word in every time.

Lenore looked at her kids as she drove. She hated this.

It had been almost a full year since her husband had passed from cancer and now, the family dynamic was rapidly falling apart. She hoped this little adventure to a cabin retreat would give them a chance to rekindle some happiness before David graduated and left for college, it was going to be a hard time for her.

Unfortunately, Carissa had to bring her boyfriend along for the trip. Kurt wasn't a bad kid, he was just arrogant, always talking and trying to sound like he was right, regardless of anyone's opinion.

To make things worse, David had decided to invite his obnoxious friend as well. Lenore didn't like Kevin. He was a loudmouth and a bum, always asking for a handout from David when he forgot something. She could just blame his parents for raising him like that, but he was eighteen and had to start taking responsibility for his own life.

So she'd just blame him for being the way he was.

She had taken two days off of work and had rented the cabin. It was a nice place from the brochure she'd seen. It was located on Mount Holcombe and placed deep in the woods of the mountain. The only warning was to bring blankets, the mountain got cold and everything had a tendency to chill when the sun went down.

Oklahoma weather was like that though.

Four seasons in one week.

Even in Elk City, they had a tendency to experience chill and blistering winds when the weather channel called for clear skies. It was a fucking tragedy really, but she tried not to dwell on it, especially since she wanted no stress while relaxing with her family.

And their hanger-ons.

Driving along the road, the road signs revealed a town up ahead at the base of the mountain and Lenore took the route to the town. It would be nice to stock up on some groceries before they hit the mountain itself. The area was located not far from Antlers, Oklahoma; so it was nice to venture along and see the natural sights as one did.

Pulling up to the first market she saw, Lenore parked the van and killed the engine, looking at everyone, "Okay y'all, time for some shopping. Don't just get junk food."

The kids nodded and everyone got out, using the sliding door to let Kurt, Carissa and Kevin out of the backseat. The group stretched their legs as they headed into the store. Lenore was wearing a pair of tan pants, white blouse and plaid overshirt. David was dressed in baggy jeans, a blue t-shirt and his letterman jacket. Kurt had dressed in his black cargo shorts, black t-shirt and black hoodie. Carissa was wearing a pair of black denim shorts, black tank-top, and also had a black hoodie covering her top. Kevin was dressed in a simple pair of jeans and long-sleeve shirt.

They were ready to get their favorite food and try to sneak something sweet in while doing it, Lenore was too lenient, they knew she'd let them get away with anything at this point.

As they entered, the group split up to go down the aisles and Lenore pushed the shopping cart alone, tossing in some pasta, flour, cooking oil, eggs and other ingredients. David and Kevin walked through the cheaper food aisle, snagging noodles, canned hash and sandwich ingredients. Carissa and Kurt, meanwhile, simply walked through the aisles without looking for anything in particular.

Carissa wasn't interested in very much. Ever since her father passed, she'd felt like she was empty and there wasn't anything she wanted to do hardly anymore. It was like her whole life had shattered and now, she only had her mom who was always working. She brushed her red bangs from her face as she looked down to her converse shoes while walking through an aisle.

Kurt was looking for snack cakes down the aisle and was letting her have some space, he knew she didn't like it when he hovered. He loved her, but her father's death had killed her and the last thing he wanted to do was make her think he was crowding her.

Carissa walked while looking down until she bumped into someone and looked up, "My fault."

The person, a tall and lumbering man with a long red beard, looked back at her, "No, it was my bad."

She looked him over. He was wearing fur around his back and had a pair of dirty overalls on, but she could tell that despite his beard, he was in his late-teens or early twenties. She smiled, "We'll blame it on this confusing store."

"Sounds about right," the man replied, putting some food in his shopping cart, "Never seen you around here. Where you from?"

"Elk City. I'm just here with my family for a sorta vacation."

"Better places to vacation than around here," the man chuckled, "Y'all heading up to Cannedy Cabin?"

"I think that's the place," Carissa shrugged. The man nodded, "Be careful; it gets pretty cold up there, you might wanna put on a pair of pants. Don't need those lovely legs freezing off."

Carissa paused; was this guy checking her out? Was he just being nice? She opened her mouth to speak until Kurt made his presence known, "Hey sweetheart, who's your new friend?"

The bearded guy looked at Kurt, standing straight as he hovered over the two, "Felton and who are you?"

"Kurt," Kurt offered his hand, but Felton did not reciprocate, Kurt withdrew his aborted handshake, "Well, I think your mom is checking out. Let's go see if she needs help."

Carissa turned to walk with Kurt, but looked over her shoulder, "It was nice to meet you."

She watched as he continued to stare at her. No doubt about it, he was watching her ass as she left, too bad he was in for a rude awakening. She was only sixteen and she was not easy, she didn't even like it when Kurt tried to be intimate with her.

Getting back to Lenore, they assisted with bagging up the items as they headed out to the car after she paid for the groceries. It was a nice little town. Charming and rustic,basically a country town in the woods. Kevin looked over to David as he waited for Kurt and Carissa to get into the car, "Kind of an eerie place. It's like something out of a hillbilly horror movie."

"Only if you think it is," David shrugged, "This is Oklahoma. Nothing weird happens here, you gotta go to West Virginia for that kind of thing, didn't you see the movies?"

"I'm just saying."

"Listen, my mom is trying to have one more weekend with us before everything goes back to depression," David looked at Kevin, "Please, keep the horror movie shit to yourself. Just try to make the trip fun, okay?"

Kevin raised his hands, "Okay, sorry, I'll keep my comments to myself."

"Thank you," David said, watching as his friend got into the van and then he did as well, watching as his mom put the van into reverse to exit the parking lot. Soon, they were back on the road and heading up the mountain trail. The woods were thick, hard to see through the trees and the whole mountain seemed to be barren.

As much as he hated to admit it, Kevin was right, this place was eerie.

THREE

Upon arriving at the cabin, the crew got out of the van and headed up to it. Lenore got a full view of the cabin from the outside.

It was a large cabin with a stone chimney that was situated on one side whilst the door was off a wooden porch. The walls were dark brown and dark red, log-cabin chic with a brown roof overhead. The windows were clear and the inside they could tell was warmly inviting. The area surrounding it was bereft of trees and included a side porch that had a grill sitting under a wooden awning.

It was quite a luxurious little setup. The cost hadn't been extortionate, especially for three bedrooms and a balcony that was located on the back upper deck. There wasn't much in the way of television or internet service on the mountain, probably due to the trees and the density of the mountain itself, if that was possible. Lenore didn't mind, she wasn't much of a phone user anyway and her kids, thankfully, knew that this was a time for making memories together.

Carissa and David assisted their mother with bringing in the groceries whilst Kurt got what was left to bring in as well. Kevin, meanwhile, milled about the side of the cabin looking around the area. It was nature. Kevin didn't like nature.

He didn't like much of anything outside of the city.

It didn't matter, he wasn't there for anything more than moral support and to enjoy two days away from the city, even if they were in the middle of nowhere on top of mount fuck-knows-where. If anything, he'd be able to catch a glimpse or two of Carissa nude thanks to the window located in the bathroom.

Small joys, he shrugged, kicking rocks on the ground.

Entering the cabin, Lenore sat the groceries on the table and smiled, taking a deep breath of the oak scent of the cabin interior. It had furnishings, a Persian rug, a fireplace that was set to go, a stairway to the top floor and some modest furniture in the living room. It was certainly a liveable place to stay for a few days.

David smiled as he took the goods out of the sacks and put them in the cabinets, he didn't mind, he liked helping his mom with unpacking. He knew his dad would have told him if he was there. David hadn't taken the death of their father as bad as Carissa had, but it had still affected him enough to wish that he could go back in time and be of more help than he originally had been.

David hadn't expected his father to die. He had expected him to beat it into remission. He wasn't thinking clearly back then and now, he wished he had done more for him. Even if it was simply cleaning him up after he got too weak to go to the toilet.

Carissa spun around as she looked around the large interior of their vacation

21

spot. She smiled, taking her hood off as she let her long red hair loose and smiled, this was just what she had been expecting. A comfy and cozy little place to relax before school started up again. She was gonna be a junior this year and it was crunch time, she wanted to succeed at school.

Her father had always told her to shoot for the moon and get past the stars, it was something she would do to honor his memory. She just had to do it.

Kurt came up behind her and rubbed her shoulders, "Pretty nice place."

"I'll say," Carissa giggled, "I'd love to live in something like this one day."

"Maybe we will," Kurt smiled, dropping subtle hints on expecting to stay with her for the rest of her life. She was a total catch and he didn't want to let go, even if she didn't feel the same way as time went on. She liked Kurt and enjoyed being with him, but the future was full of different paths, so she wasn't making long-term investments in relationships right now. Besides, she still wanted to do so much before tying any knots.

Lenore finished putting up everything with David's help and turned to everyone, "So, what should we do first?"

"I think a hike would be cool," David smiled, tossing a couple of chips in his mouth. Carissa shook her head, "Nah, lets just lounge and be lazy."

"I've been sitting for four hours," David groaned, "I want to go for a walk in the woods."

"Nobody's stopping you," Carissa waved him off and turned to speak to Kurt, earning a look of annoyance from her brother. Lenore sighed, "Okay, how about Carissa stays and lounges and I'll go hiking with David. Later, I'll make dinner and we can all play a game afterwards, sound good?"

Carissa sighed, "Yeah, sure, sounds great."

Lenore nodded, taking a heavy sigh, she really wanted a group activity. Something to start it off right. Now, she was essentially splitting up everyone to do different things. She felt her will starting to break but she paused, keeping herself intact as she considered the fact there were two days to spend with them.

Maybe they would slowly come together as the hours passed?

Lenore took her bag and headed to the master bedroom, setting the bags on the bed and sat after she did, looking down as she rubbed her eyes. Fucking Daniel, why did he have to leave and make her a single mother? They had promised to be together forever and now, she was a widow with two older kids, unable to get them to do something together. It was a fucking tragedy, like everything else, she hated the loneliness.

Meanwhile, David walked over to Carissa, "Can I talk to you?"

Carissa sighed, turning to look at him, "What?"

"Alone?" David shot a dirty look at Kurt. Kurt raised his hands, walking backwards, "Sure, don't let me get in the way of your melodrama, Dave."

Carissa watched as Kurt headed out of

the cabin and turned to David, putting her hands on her hips, "Why can't you be nicer to Kurt? He's a good person."

"He's a cunt," David huffed, "Listen, mom is counting on us to make this a good trip. We need to do our part. Even if you don't want to do something, just pretend like you do and try to make things easier for her."

"Who do you think you're talking to?" Carissa cocked her eyebrow at him, "You're not my father, David, you don't get to tell me what to do. You're gonna be gone come August and I'm gonna be stuck at home with mom, so don't try to boss me around like when we were kids."

"You still are a kid," David crossed his arms, "Act like a fucking adult and try to make this trip easier on mom. Or else."

"Or else what?"

"Or else I'll beat your ass," David threatened, "And I'll kill Kurt if he gets in the way. Enough of the spoiled princess shit, Rissa, time to grow the fuck up."

Carissa gritted her teeth, anger making her shake as she shoved him aside and walked out of the cabin, slamming the door. David watched as she left and turned to see his mom coming out of her room, now dressed in a pair of hiking boots, she looked at him, "Where'd Carissa go off to?"

"I think she wants to go on the hike," David smiled, smugly. He knew she'd probably bitch the whole time, but he didn't care. He was going to make their mom happy and let her know they had her best interests at heart, regardless if he had to kick ass along the way. He was the man of the house now and had to act the part, even if he was off to a bad start.

He didn't want it to be like this, but unfortunately, life had thrown them a curve ball and he was stuck in it. He didn't have the heart to tell his mom he was going to stay home instead of go to college and do his best to help support the family, he would tell her after they got back to the city.

For now, he was just going to try to bring them together if he could. He had to. They were a broken family and his father would have wanted him to try to hold them together. It wasn't going to be an easy task but this was his burden to bear.

Opening the door for Lenore, he smiled, "Let's go see if we can find Bigfoot."

FOUR

Kevin walked past the cabin and into the thicket of trees, looking around to find any discernible path through which to walk. He had heard about paths made by Indians or some shit long ago, so there should be some kind of trail made on the mountains.

He walked along, looking through the trees as he went, they really were thick to look through. The leaves were green and the pine needles were all over the place, it made any paths hard to find and that was something he was not hoping for. He continued to walk and spoke aloud to himself, muttering lyrics to a song he had heard earlier that day.

Soon, he found himself coming to the sound of other people.

He turned over his shoulder, thinking he

might have heard David or Carissa talking, but he saw nothing. It was kind of odd. He could hear voices but couldn't see anyone through the barrage of trees around him.

Shit, he thought to himself, maybe the schizophrenia was hitting him like it did to his old man in prison. Shaking his head, he continued to walk as the voices grew a little more clear. It was women talking. They sounded like they were having fun. Plus, there was the sound of splashing as though water was involved.

Reaching out to move some limbs from his view, he caught sight of where the voices were originating from and smiled.

A group of women were swimming in a small pond that was hidden in the woods. The women were naked. Their bare flesh was a sight for him to feast upon. They had large breasts, long thin legs and round bums that were shining in the sunlight. He stood still, watching the women laugh and talk and smoke what appeared to be joints.

Other vacationers on the mountain, who would have guessed? Maybe there was another cabin nearby?

Sliding his hand in his pants, he fondled himself as he watched the group of bare hotties splash about in the pond. It was a hot spring or something, judging by the steam that was rising off the surface. Stepping forward a bit, Kevin slipped and rolled forward down the small mound, rolling off onto his back mere feet from the spring.

The women turned to see and caught sight of him lying on his back, giggling among themselves. One woman called out, "Hey there!"

Kevin raised up, dazed and leaves stuck in his shaggy hair, he waved despite his blushing red face. Another woman called to him, "You have any pot?"

"Not on me," Kevin replied, standing up to brush himself off, "Where are y'all from?"

"Broken Bow, you?"

"Elk City," he replied, walking towards them and hoping they didn't see the boner in his pants. He made his way until he was at the bank of the spring and crouched down,

"I'm Kevin McNally."

The woman that had asked about the weed nodded, not shamed in the least that she was topless and had warm water dripping off her swollen nipples, "I'm Ariana."

She reached out to shake his hand and Kevin did the same, only for her to pull him down into the waters. Abruptly getting a noseful of warm spring water, Kevin shot up and broke through the surface, "Well, that was unexpected."

Another woman kicked over to him, holding him close, "You're kind of cute, Kevin, I'm Breanna. The other whores are Stacy and June."

Stacy and June, at their own side of the spring, simply shot a pair of middle fingers at Breanna. Kevin smiled, "Okay, nice, nice, are y'all on vacation?"

"Definitely," Breanna giggled, her breasts rubbing against Kevin's shoulder, "You?"

"I'm here with some friends," Kevin shrugged, "Not my ideal place to vacay, but it's starting to look a lot better now."

Breanna giggled, "You should get out of those wet clothes and let your freak flag fly, besides, you looked like you were excited to find us. Doing a bit of peeping?"

Kevin blushed, "Well, you know."

"Honey, just ask," Breanna giggled, obviously very stoned at this point, "We'll do anything you want. But you gotta join the rest of us."

Kevin instantly pulled his clothes off, tossing the wet garments off to the side and sunk under the water, the warmth overcoming him as he stripped totally naked. Breanna reached down, taking a hold of his pole and began to play with it, licking in his ear as he felt himself getting steamed up.

Stacy and June, meanwhile, were making out with each other. They were obviously very interested in each other's intimacy as Ariana waded over to give Kevin a hit of the joint in her fingers. Kevin nodded, his vacation was definitely picking up, especially as he felt himself worked to release in the waters of the spring.

Breanna giggled, "You came faster than I expected."

Kevin chuckled, feeling the effects of the marijuana overcoming him, "Well, I blame you, plus your friends certainly didn't help."

Breanna laughed and Ariana laughed, Kevin wrapping his arms around their backs as he relaxed in the water. Shit, he knew this was gonna be a long and fun two days. He would definitely get some pussy while hanging with them. Fuck David and his sister, they were nothing compared to this.

Ariana took a hard drag on the weed and blew the smoke out, "So, who's down for an orgy?"

"Me," Breanna raised her hand; the women were very clearly not in the right state of mind, but it didn't matter to Kevin. He was only out to get laid by the babes in the water. It was something out of a porno and he didn't mind in the slightest. Breanna leaned in to whisper in his ear, "Can you handle all four of us?"

"I can try," Kevin giggled, instantly being hit by a splash of something warm and wet all over the side of his face. Damn, he thought, this chick's kinky. He rarely liked being spit on, but she was quite a spitter as he turned to face her. Breanna was staring at him, blood running from her nose as he noticed an arrow resting right through her head. The tip hanging out of her left ear and blood running off of it into the water.

Kevin instantly moved away from her as the other girls started screaming, Ariana screamed, "What the fuuu-" suddenly catching a pickaxe through the back of her head and the pick coming out of her mouth, knocking her teeth into the pull. Kevin looked up to see two large men, dressed in overalls, standing at the bank of the spring.

He turned to swim away from them, wading as he attempted to find footing to stand on and moved towards June and Stacy as they tried clamoring out of the spring towards their red panel van. Kevin called to them, "Wait for me!"

Suddenly, a hard object hit Kevin in the back of the head and knocked him forward into a daze, the object shattering as it cracked into his skull. It was some form of whiskey bottle, emptied and the label floated on the top of the water. Kevin, his head gushing blood, could only watch as Stacy caught a flying hatchet to the face, knocking her on her back to bleed out.

One of the men slapped June to the ground and leapt onto her, savagely dislocating her shoulders to keep her from fighting back as he pulled her naked screaming body into the woods. He raised his hand as he tried to will himself to help Stacy as her body writhed in death throes from the hatchet sticking out of her face.

The other large man reached down, ripping the hatchet from her head and moved over to Kevin, standing over him from the bank of the spring. Kevin couldn't speak or move hardly, his head was seeping blood into the water. His mind brutally dazed from the force of the bottle shattering into his skull.

Swinging the hatched down, the man buried the blade into the base of Kevin's neck from behind. The chop severed Kevin's spine and rendered him completely motionless, falling forward into the water. The man smiled, putting the hatchet on his belt and moved his right boot to push down on Kevin's back, submerging his paralyzed body under the water until he would inevitably drown.

Kevin's lungs burned as he tried holding his breath, but alas, there was no hope. He couldn't move or fight or get free; he could only accept his fate as his chest filled with water and his mind went blank before death overtook him.

FIVE

Walking through the woods; Lenore, David, Carissa and Kurt didn't say much to each other and primarily focused on leaving markers for the lack of a worn trail.

Carissa looked through the trees, admiring how large they were and how hidden the sky seemed to be due to the branches filled with leaves. She looked at Kurt, "This is such a fun time. I'd much rather be doing this than sitting on a sofa and relaxing."

David rolled his eyes as they walked, "Hey mom, what was that song that Dad always wanted to sing when we went walking?"

Lenore shook her head, smiling slightly, "I don't really recall."

"I think it was 'Row Row Row Your Boat'

or something like that," David shrugged, "Not much of a song to sing while walking though."

Their father, God rest his soul, was not the brightest when it came to coming up with fun activities to do. He liked to sing and he liked to dance, but other than that, he was kind of shit at picking songs they could appreciate. Still, it would be nice to hear him sing just one more time before anything else happened on the trip.

Lenore paused, looking around and nodded, "I'd say this mountain is pretty far up. Maybe we should turn back? I don't think we'll reach the top before nightfall."

"I agree," Carissa chimed in, "Some guy at the store said this place gets really cold at night. Not exactly something I want to test out."

"Maybe if you put clothes on," David snorted. Carissa turned to sneer at him, "We're on vacation. I dressed in shorts because that's what you wear when you're on vacation. Kurt's wearing shorts, too."

David laughed, "Yeah, well, thankfully, I

can't see all of Kurt's legs. You are showing off way too much skin for the woods."

Carissa rolled her eyes, "Can we please just go back to the cabin? I don't want to freaking walk anymore. I'm tired."

Lenore nodded, "Yeah, that's probably for the best, we need to get dinner started anyway. Maybe tomorrow we can try to go up to the top. What do you guys think?"

David looked up to view the top of Mount Holcombe, nodding, "Seems doable."

"Like you can judge the distance," Carissa rolled her eyes and turned around to walk back the way they came. Kurt followed behind her. Lenore looked at David, "Can you please not argue with her, please, let's just try to make this fun."

"It's not my fault," David sighed, "I told her she needs to grow up."

"I think we all need to grow up," Lenore replied, walking after her daughter towards the cabin. David watched as they walked away, looking down at the ground beneath him and around the woods. So much for a fun hiking experience. Still, dinner sounded good and he wanted to help as much as he could, so no harm in getting back to the cabin to prepare for a meal.

After reaching the cabin, Carissa sat on the sofa and Kurt sat next to her, both talking about the annoyance on the hiking trip. Kurt was starting to get more and more irritated with the way that David was treating his sister. It was unbecoming of a guy to be so mean to someone so fragile.

He had to stand up for her soon or else, she was gonna beat David to a bloody pulp. He had seen her kickboxing classes and knew she was a force to be reckoned with. He was certainly not going to go toe to toe with her.

She sighed, "I just want to try to enjoy the vacation. Is that so hard to ask? Am I wanting too much of life?"

" No," Kurt replied, "There's never anything wrong with wanting to relax, especially after the hardship you guys have been through. You deserve it."

"Try telling my brother that."

"Don't worry," Kurt held her close,

putting his arm around her, "I'm gonna talk to him soon enough."

In the kitchen, David prepped the pans as Lenore got the fish out to prepare and season. It was a rustic tradition to eat fish while in the woods. She remembered when her grandparents used to do the same thing for her when she was younger. They instilled a lot of appreciation for nature in her.

If only they could see her now. She was a true pioneer woman, even if she lived in a townhouse in Elk City and rarely went into the woods, okay maybe pioneer woman was a step too far. She still had the mindset of one.

Especially now that Daniel was gone and she had to raise her kids alone, pioneer women went through the same thing all the time. It was hardship that taught you how to embrace the path life throws you one. Regardless of how it happened, it happened and there wasn't anything she could do about it now.

Daniel had been her anchor and now, she was essentially adrift. David helped as a son could, but there were things she still needed that he couldn't give, like affection and a shoulder to cry on and a mind full of wisdom far beyond his own. She hated it. She hated being alone.

She looked over to see Carissa and Kurt cuddling on the couch. She was happy for them, but she missed it herself, she missed having her childhood sweetheart holding her close to keep her safe from the hatred of the universe. It was something she didn't think she would ever overcome, no matter how long she tried or what she did.

Putting the fish in the pan over the burner, she continued to drop seasonings on it and then moved to put biscuits in the oven, ensuring there would be quite a small feast for the kids to enjoy.

David, meanwhile, was running all over the cabin and outside as the sun had begun to set. He came back in, "Anyone seen Kevin?"

Carissa shook her head, "He might have gotten lost."

"God fucking forbid," David groaned.

Lenore turned around, "David, watch your mouth!"

"Sorry mom," David sighed. It wasn't like Kevin to be gone for so long. He thought the guy might have decided to stay behind at the cabin when they went on their hike. Now, he was wondering where he was. The guy was his best friend and he didn't want to be stuck for two days with just fucking Kurt as the only guy in the cabin with him. He went outside into the darkened woods, calling out, "Kevin! Kevin! Kev! Stop fucking around and come eat!"

No sign of him.

David ventured a bit further out, feeling a cold chill overcome him as the temperature started to decrease sharply, "Kev! Seriously man, come eat some dinner! Where are you!"

Nothing.

David groaned, fuck. Walking back into the cabin, he looked around at everyone, "I can't find him."

"I'm sure he'll be back soon," Lenore attempted to placate her son, "Maybe he just went out on his own hike and got too far out, you both were in the boy scouts, so he knows to leave trail markers behind."

"It's freaking cold out there," David shivered, walking over to start the fireplace up and get some flames going. He stood over it as the flames slowly built up over the log in the fireplace and looked at the mantle, some pictures. Grabbing one of the frames, he looked at the family, big burly guys with a pair of smaller girls and an older couple that looked ready to bite the head off of anyone who came up to them. Setting it back on the mantle, he noticed a book that looked interesting, a horror book.

Shit, maybe Kevin was right, maybe others had similar ideas about the cabin. It was for sure creepy and cold in the woods. Lenore spoke up, "Dinner's ready. Come to the table."

Carissa and Kurt got off the couch, walking towards the table and took a seat. David turned and walked over to the kitchen himself, helping Lenore put the food out for everyone. Hopefully Kevin got back soon, everything looked so damn good and he was certain that nothing would be left.

He caught sight of Kurt looking at him with an annoyed set of eyes. David shook his head and took a seat, doing his best to avoid a staring contest.

Kurt was such a fucking cunt.

<u>SIX</u>

The fish was put on their plates, along with biscuits, some vegetable concoction and some fried potatoes. The family ate in silence as the sound of the wind picking up outside whistled from beyond the windows.

Lenore looked up, chewing her food as she watched her kids eating and wiped her mouth, "So, what do you think? Can I cook or can I cook?"

"You can definitely cook," David replied. Carissa rolled her eyes, mumbling, "Kiss ass."

David looked up at her, "Come again?"

Carissa shook her head, looking at Lenore, "Food's great, mom. We really enjoy it."

David chuckled, earning a look of ire from his sister and her boyfriend. Carissa tilted her head, "Something funny?"

"Are you speaking for both of you now?" David looked at the two, "When are you going to morph into one person?"

Kurt dropped his fork, sitting back and crossed his arms; he was finished with David's insults. He shook his head, "Dude, show some respect for your sister, don't you think she's having a hard enough time?"

"I'm sorry," David looked up at him, "Did someone ask for your opinion? I don't remember anyone saying, 'Kurt, please, grace us with your bullshit'."

Lenore sighed as Carissa growled, "Don't talk down to him. At least he knows how to be respectful."

David laughed, clearing his throat, it was too easy for her to make this about herself. It was just the way Carissa was. Even as kids, she was a spoiled brat and he was the one who had to watch her get her way. They were older now and she was still the same way, though now she had a guy wanting to take her side over everything. David spoke to her, "That's not respect, Rissa, that's called being a bitch."

"Whoa," Kurt leaned forward, "Who are you calling a bitch, David? At least I'm here for her when she's upset. You just tell her to suck it up."

"Yeah, no shit," David crossed his arms, "Eventually, you two are gonna have to grow up and learn that life is full of sadness. Maybe you'll figure that out when she kicks your dumbass to the curb."

Lenore rubbed her forehead, trying to eat in peace, utterly annoyed at the bickering going on at the table. Carissa slammed her fist on the table, "Back off, David, you don't think I know life is full of sadness? I helped Dad when he was weak and when the cancer had spread to his brain, I wiped his ass. You didn't do anything but play it off as nothing. You're a shitty brother and an even shittier son."

David gnashed his teeth, "At least I'm trying to make up for it now. You're just wallowing in your self-pity. You don't deserve to sit at this table or be part of this family, we're trying to move on and you're making it about you. You need to stop being a spoiled cunt and your bitch needs to eat outside with the rest of the dogs."

Kurt, shaking in his seat as he heard Carissa's voice crack in a whimper, quickly reached out to grab David's collar and threw him to the floor. David fell to the wooden floor as Kurt got on top of him, pummeling him in the face and stomach, Carissa quickly got out of her chair and walked backwards. Lenore joined Carissa and yelled at them, "Stop it, now! Fucking stop it!"

David reached up and grabbed ahold of Kurt's hair, swinging him down to the ground, giving David the chance to take the upper hand. David's fist smashed into Kurt's bloody face three vicious times before Carissa finally ran over and yanked David backwards to the floor, jumping between them, "I said fucking stop!"

Both men, adrenaline running fast whilst their faces bled from busted noses and cut lips, gasped for air as they tried to calm their nerves. Kurt nodded, rubbing the blood from his face, "Okay baby, I'm done."

"Pussy," David spat, turning to wrench open the door and instantly came face to face with a woman covered in a bearskin. He paused, "Um, hello?"

The woman, shivering in the cold wind, pulled the bearskin tighter around her body and spoke to him, "I need your help!"

Lenore came over beside David and looked at the woman, "I'm Lenore Stone and this is my son, David. Who are you? Why are you out in the woods so late?"

"I'm Roon," the woman spoke, shivering as she looked around anxiously, "I need your help. There are people coming after me."

"Who?" David asked, unaware that Kurt and Carissa had come up behind him to look at the stranger as well. The woman was young, probably fifteen or sixteen, had long auburn hair and was visibly naked under the bearskin. She had no shoes on. She looked like she hadn't washed in a while.

The girl, Roon, shook her head, "There's no time to explain. Please, can I come in? I need your help."

Lenore nodded, nudging David aside, "Yes, please come in and warm yourself by the fire."

The girl entered the cabin, quickly went to the fireplace and opened her bearskin covering, letting the warmth of the flames waft over her body. David, his nose bleeding, wiped his face and looked at Lenore, "We should find out where she's from. I can drive her back to her cabin."

"I don't think there are any other cabins around here," Lenore said, watching the girl warming herself up. She walked over to Roon and asked, "Are you hungry? We have dinner ready if you're hungry or need anything."

Roon turned to Lenore and shook her head, covering herself back up, "No, but I am telling you. We need to leave. There are people coming after me and they won't stop until they get me back, dead or alive."

"Who?" Lenore asked, hands on her hips as Carissa whispered to Kurt and David watched from where he stood. Roon shook her head, "The mountain folk. They live up here and they kill everyone they can get their hands on, they eat people, they rape and murder them and then, they fucking eat them!"

David immediately went to the drawer and pulled out a steak knife, "How far back are they?"

"Huh?" Roon looked at him, tilting her head, "They are not far. They may be here now!"

The door swung open as a large man came running in, holding up a pickaxe and swung it down, narrowly missing Carissa as Kurt tackled her out of the way. The man raised the weapon, looking at the kids as he smiled, his teeth a filthy gold and hanging from his jaw was a long bushy red beard. The man was wearing a cow skull over the top of his head and his clothing was fashioned from animal skins.

Lenore grabbed one of the picture frames from the mantle and threw it, hitting the man in the back of the head.

Roon quickly punched Lenore in the lower part of her back so she stumbled backwards and then dropped to all fours, causing the older woman to trip as she stumbled backwards. The man turned and swung the pickaxe down, the pick going through Lenore's right arm and into the wooden floor. Lenore screamed out in utter pain and agony; David gripped the knife handle, running quickly to leap onto the large man.

With a hard slam, he buried the blade of the knife into the man's back, forcing him to release the handle of the pickaxe as he raised up in pain. Kurt ran up to throw punches at the large man while Carissa tackled Roon to the floor, turning to pull the pick out of her screaming mother. The opened door blew in wind that caused a chill to overcome the warmth of the cabin.

Suddenly two more large men in similar outfits as the assailant, ventured into the cabin and moved to aid the man overcome by David and Kurt. One of the men, the top of his head boasting a coon skin cap, grabbed a hold of David in a headlock. David struggled as the man applied enough pressure to force him to grow limp and pass out, nothing more than a body in the man's arms.

The other man went over and sent a huge fist into the side of Kurt's head, knocking him cold in one swing. Carissa had Lenore raised up and was watching the scene as the men took Kurt and David towards the door; Carissa attempted to stop them, but shared the same massive punch as her boyfriend had, the impact knocking her into the coffee table that fell to pieces.

Roon raised up and looked down at Carissa, holding a previously hidden hook against the girl's neck as she looked at Lenore, "Come willingly or I'll kill her, here and now."

"Don't harm my babies," Lenore cried out, her right arm limp and bloody from the pickaxe wound. The three large men simply laughed as the one who had been stabbed reached down and grabbed Lenore by her hair, dragging her along as they exited the cabin. They would send their younger brother back for the daughter, whistling for

Roon to follow them into the cold night.

Carissa lay still on the smashed remains of the coffee table as the wind continued to blow in from outside and instill the cabin with a growing sense of dread.

SEVEN

David woke slowly, opening his eyes as he found himself in a cramped position within a confined space, his hands and ankles bound with some form of leather straps. His nose and lip had ceased bleeding, but they were still sore and he was certain he'd have a black eye or bruise on his face.

He looked over in the dimly lit area to see Kurt lying beside him, equally bound and still unconscious, he sighed. No sign of his mother or his sister, he realized. Looking around, he made out that he was in some kind of metal cage that was only meant to hold a very large wolf or something. The cage was in a large room that had an overhead lamp providing very poor lighting.

He spoke out, "Hello?"

He heard nothing. He spoke again,

"Hello?!"

Suddenly, the sound of a door opened and footsteps could be heard as though descending an unseen staircase. FInally, a large figure appeared from the entrance that was out of view. It was one of the men who had abducted them.

David coughed, "Where am I? Who the fuck are you?"

The man walked over to the cage and patted it, smiling, "You're in my cellar."

"Cellar? Why have you brought us here? Who are you people?"

The man reached over to a mini-fridge and pulled out a plate of something, he then turned to David, "You're here for food."

"Food?"

The man smiled, opening the top of the cage and dumped the plate into the cage, covering David and Kurt in strips of rotting meat. The smell was foul and the meat was covered in maggots, the little worms crawling over the two of them. David cussed as he attempted to wipe the meat and white worms off of himself, the movements forced Kurt to wake while moaning in pain. The man laughed as he watched David struggling, it was something he had seen dozens of times, yet he continued to enjoy it.

He crouched in front of the cage, staring at David and Kurt, "You boys done trespassed on the wrong property. Now, y'all are gonna learn the true meaning of private property."

"We didn't trespass," David growled, "You fuckers broke in and kidnapped us, now, I demand you let us go or I'm calling the cops."

The man laughed, raised up and cracked his knuckles, "If I let you out of that cage, you're gonna wish like hell that you'd stay inside forever. I been known to tear people in half with my bare hands."

"Where's my girlfriend?" Kurt mumbled, his face severely gashed open from the punch and the swelling made it hard to speak clearly. The man chuckled, "She got a fine pair of legs on her. Don't you worry, we gonna put her to good use, she gonna be given a brood of babies to raise in time. The other one's too old, she gonna have to die."

David screamed, shaking the cage, "No! You fucking hillbilly motherfucker, let me the fuck out of here, I'll beat you to death if you touch either of them!"

The sound of the door opening and footsteps broke through the noise as someone else entered the cellar. It was a small old lady, dressed in a long simple dress and her hands visibly ruined by some form of arthritis. She came up to them, shoving the big guy aside and looked down in the cage, "I never heard such profanity in my house! You shut your trap, youngster, before I pull you out of that cage and cut your tongue out!"

"Who are the fuck you?" Kurt asked, holding his swollen face. The old lady sneered at him, her face a mess of drooping skin and wrinkles, she fixed her glasses and said, "Mama Cannedy and I won't have no swearin' in my home! You boys best learn to respect my house or as the Lord said in First Peter three-ten: He whoever loveth life shall have no evil from his tongue!"

David and Kurt looked at each other and then turned back to Mama Cannedy, nodding.

The old woman turned to look at the big man, "Get them cleaned up for supper. I don't want no crying of being hungry in my house, they either eat or they die, your daddy can't handle no loud noises."

"Yes mama," the man nodded, watching as she slowly exited the cellar and then he turned back to them, "Y'all think you're scared of me? You never seen what that old lady can do with an axe. Oh," he turned to David, "And to answer your question, I'm Carver Cannedy."

They watched as Carver exited the cellar and then David looked at Kurt, "We gotta get the fuck out of here."

"Dude, how? This cage is tiny and we're tied up, plus those guys are huge. I hope Carissa's okay."

"Yeah," David nodded, "Me too. But we can only hope she got away. We need to come up with a plan and make it work, we need to save my mom."

Kurt groaned, attempting to raise up as his face nudged against David's shoulder and he whimpered from the pain. He couldn't get Carissa off his mind. He didn't care if he didn't make it, he only cared about her and was hopeful that she wasn't in the clutches of these people. She would never settle for being a slave or a captive, she was headstrong and stubborn, which he liked about her.

David thought in his mind as he considered a plan of action.

They were supposed to get cleaned up and brought up for supper, whatever that consisted of. Judging by the stench of the meat and the overwhelming amount of maggots in the meat, it wasn't hard to assume what supper was going to be made of. He just hoped that his mom hadn't been turned into supper already.

Kevin was right all along, this was a horror show in the making and now, he wasn't here to see just how right he was. Maybe he had gone for help?

The thoughts were dashed when he looked over to see Kevin's clothes in a pile near a 55-gallon drum that had blood running down the sides of it from the top. He felt his heart sink as he realized that Kevin never got away. Kevin must have been taken earlier before they had settled down for dinner.

Maybe even before they went on their hike.

He looked at Kurt, "Okay, listen up, I'm not gonna say this more than once. I have an idea about how we can get the hell out of here and preferably, in one piece."

"I'm down," Kurt nodded, lending his ear as David went into detail about the plan that he had cooked up suddenly. It seemed doable. It seemed like something they could possibly get away with. The only problem on Kurt's mind was Carissa.

What about his beloved girlfriend?

Was she safe?

Was she alive?

He couldn't help but wonder. He hated not knowing. Especially now, when everything was looking grim, he hated not being able to know if she was safe.

He had to will himself to agree to David's plan. It was the only way to stay positive.

EIGHT

Carissa lay where she had fallen, her face swollen from the clobbering punch and her eyes slowly fluttering open, instantly realizing how painful her face was.

Her entire body hurt. The tumble into the coffee table had left her feeling limp as she looked around slowly at everything; the table still had food on it, the fire was dying down in the fireplace and a cold air had settled in the cabin. Before she could raise up, she heard the sound of footsteps on the porch and she quickly closed her eyes, doing her best to appear unconscious.

Felton Cannedy entered the cabin and moved to the table, reaching down to eat the fish that was still in the pan, shoveling it in his mouth. He then turned to the girl on the floor laying atop a pile of broken wood.

He looked down at her, he'd seen her earlier that day, at the store.

He didn't remember if he caught her name or what it was if she had told him, but he did remember how polite she was.

His brothers had already finished taking everyone else and had left him the job of taking her back to the family home, pretty simple work. Felton was a straggler, hardly ever coming along with them whenever they went hunting at the cabin for whoever was staying there.

Leaning down, he pulled her to lay flat on her back and took a second to look her over. She was wearing shorts, a hoodie, black and white shoes and her hair was red as embers in the fireplace. Felton licked his lips as he hovered over her. She was too pretty for him to resist and before long, he had pulled his tan trousers down and lay atop of her, forcing her shorts down as he prepared himself to take her.

Carissa opened her eyes a crack to see the man hovering over her. She instantly recognized him. It was the guy she bumped into at the store, Felton. Perhaps he had come to rescue her. Her thoughts of rescue were dashed as she felt him enter her and she opened her eyes immediately, attempting to push him off of her.

Felton struggled as he attempted to push her arms down, "Don't struggle, darling, I don't want to hurt you none."

She screamed, "Get off of me! Please, don't do this!"

The large man refused to obey as she screamed and continuously struggled, yet he continued his assault on her body, his large force overwhelmed her as she cried out in pain. Felton simply continued and worked himself against her, he'd done it before, the pleasure was too great to ever ignore.

Carissa cried and screamed and struggled to no avail. The man was too large for her to fight back or get away from, she could only look away towards the door while he forced her body to his will. With a hearty bellow, Felton finished within her and raised up, pulling up his trousers. He looked down at her, "I wish I could have you to myself, but I can't. You gotta come with me."

Reaching down, Felton pulled her up by her arms and she cried out as the pain in her body overwhelmed her. The large hillbilly threw her up on his shoulder and headed out of the cabin, but not before dousing the fireplace with the pitcher of sweet tea on the table. The effects of orgasm were still swarming his mind, but he couldn't let it get to him, he had to get back to the house before supper or he'd miss out.

Walking through the woods, the cold air hit Carissa's exposed skin and pricked with the sharp chill.

She lay hanging over his shoulder, her body frail and injured, now, her lower half was practically numb. The events played in her head over and over again, making her realize it had all been a trap from the start.

The guy had bumped into her at the store and she'd told him about staying at the cabin, though he played it off as nothing. Then that fucking girl in the bearskin had made them drop their guard by acting like she was victim. It was all a grand scheme. She whimpered, "Where are you taking me?"

"I'm taking you home," Felton replied, moving through the cold woods as he trudged the path, "You don't wanna miss supper. Mama won't like it if you don't get a proper meal in you before you start."

"Start what?" Carissa inquired, trying to find the strength to get up and off of the man, but her body utterly weakened by the assault and the rape. She didn't like the way anything sounded. She didn't want to get taken to somewhere she couldn't get away from, especially since he was taking her deeper and deeper into the woods of the mountain.

Felton rubbed the back of her thigh with his hand as he held her against him, "Before you start having babies."

"Babies?" Carissa repeated, instantly realizing what he was talking about and she quickly used all of her strength to pound her fists into his back, "Let me down! Let me go! Fuck you, fuck you, fuck you!"

Felton just smiled as he found himself walking towards the all-familiar path through the thicker part of the woods. He must have brought dozens of bodies through these woods at all hours of the night. Being the youngest brother meant he was forced to do all the dirty work, such as disposing of skeletons, dead meat and rotten flesh barrels. Ever since his father had died, the oldest brother, Cleatus, had taken over as head of the family. Papa was still alive, but he was too old to really lead the hunting party anymore.

Mount Holcombe had been the family's property since before the Civil War and they kept it so, making sure that no matter who was renting the cabin they would find themselves in boiling water. The thought of flesh boiled in water suddenly made his stomach growl, human stew was one of the best meals Mama made and it was his favorite.

An old Cannedy recipe.

He squeezed Carissa's thigh as he approached the large house, "You best shut up and not say a cuss word, Mama is a hard Christian woman and she will sew your mouth shut if you dare swear in her house. Now, are you gonna behave?"

Carissa sighed, looking down to see that they were on a porch and nodded, "Fine, I won't swear."

Felton opened the door and pulled Carissa off of him, setting her on her feet as he pulled her arms behind her to remain his captive. She looked around the inside of the large house, noticing that it was in disrepair and would be condemned if it was in the city. She saw an old man sitting in a rocking chair, listening to a radio while one of the large guys from earlier was busy cleaning blood from a pickaxe.

Suddenly, a little old lady appeared from another room and her shrill voice filled the air, "Felton! Is this the girl you was squawking about?"

"Yes, Mama," Felton replied, "This is her."

Carissa looked at the old lady, narrowing her eyes as the lady looked her over and nodded, "She's a bit too thin, definitely needs fattening up before she gets a Cannedy baby in her."

Carissa growled, "Where is my mom? Where is my boyfriend and my brother? Tell me!"

The old lady swung her hand and slapped Carissa across the swollen part of her face, forcing her to scream from the pain. Mama Cannedy shook her head and lifted a misshapen bony finger at her, "Don't you be asking nothing, little girl. You and your family done crossed a line; they're gonna pay the price and you ain't getting out of it like them. So unless you wanna die as painful as them, I tell you to shut up now," Mama then turned and yelled up the stairs to the second level, "Girls! Get your little behinds down here, now!"

The sound of footsteps coming down the stairs caught Carissa's attention as the bearskin-clothed bitch and another equally-dressed girl came down from the top of the stairs. The one from earlier, Roon, asked, "Yeah Mama?"

Mama looked at them, "Take this piece

of trash upstairs and get her cleaned up, make her pretty like the two of you."

The other girl nodded, smiling brightly with her rotten teeth, "Yes ma'am."

Before Carissa could say anything, the two girls took her arms and pulled her up the stairs to the second level of rooms. The floor was filthy and the walls had holes in them, the entire house looked ready to collapse in on itself. Roon pulled Carissa aside and said, "Listen, you don't say nothing when you go to supper, you just smile and accept everything. Me and Amethyst are working on a plan to get out of here."

Carissa sneered, "You tricked my family. You even tried to kill my mother. Where is she? Where is my momma?"

The other girl, Amethyst, pulled Carissa to one of the rooms and opened the door. Carissa's jaw dropped as she saw Lenore chained with her arms in the air and her body stripped naked, various cuts had been made to her. She was alive, but only barely and without help, not much longer. Carissa turned and quickly slapped Roon across the face, "Fuck you."

Roon gripped Carissa's neck and prepared to squeeze, but Amethyst pulled her off, whispering to her. Roon then looked at Carissa, "You'll pay for that. But for now, we need to get you ready for supper. Stop messing around and listen to me, your life is on the line."

Carissa looked at her mother and then back to Roon, she sighed. It could just be another trap. But at this point, what did it matter?

NINE

Carver and his brother, Darius, made their way down the steps into the cellar of the Cannedy Home to retrieve the two guys they had caged within.

Darius looked into the cellar as they reached the bottom and saw the two in the cage, he smiled, cackling out in a thick accent, "Well, howdy boys! Glad to see y'all are up and at em. We gotta get you all prepped for supper."

Carver rolled his eyes, "I done told 'em about supper. Help me get 'em out of the cage so we can clean 'em up."

Kurt and David remained sitting in the cramped cage, looking at the two hulking mountain men coming towards them, they were stoic and unconcerned with the possibility of this being their doom. David looked up as Carver hovered over the cage, "We'll come on one condition. You tell us where my sister is."

Darius laughed, shaking his head as Carver simply stared down at David. Carver spoke solemnly, "She's upstairs with our sisters. Don't worry your pretty little head, you'll see her at supper and get to say your goodbyes."

Kurt looked up, "How do we know you're telling the truth?"

"You callin' me a liar?" Carver leaned down to sneer at Kurt. David rolled his eyes, "Okay, let's get this over with."

"Wise decision," Darius piped up, walking over to open the cage and reached down to pull David out, using both hands as the captive was still bound. Carver reached in and grabbed Kurt by his long hair, pulling him up as well, earning several grunts of pain from him. After throwing both to the floor, the brothers took out a rag and some water, intent on cleaning the dried blood from David and Kurt's faces.

The dirty rag smeared water and filth all

over David's face, the meaty hand forcing it to scrub his scabbing blood raw from his face. David groaned as he did, but didn't say or do anything, knowing he had to play it cool.

Darius, meanwhile, had his hand rubbing all over Kurt's swollen face and earned several whimpers from him. Darius chuckled, "Come on, boy, little pain never hurt nobody."

Carver shook his head, "That boy's got longer hair than his girlfriend. Kinda makes you wonder, don't it?"

Darius laughed, caressing the side of Kurt's face, "He's sure thin enough to be a woman. Let's take a look and see if he's got something to prove it."

David watched as Darius began to pull down Kurt's shorts and Kurt yelled, "No!" lifting his legs up to kick Darius in the crotch. Kurt rolled onto his stomach and began attempting to push himself up, despite David's repeated orders to stop. Carver didn't do anything but watch as Kurt got to his feet and started hopping towards the stairway, only for Darius to instantly tackle him to the floor, sending several punches into his ribs.

Kurt yelled out in pain; the sound of his ribs cracking and the punches landing filled the stale air of the cellar. Carver laughed, "He sure sounds like a girl. Maybe you need to teach him a lesson about his place in the world."

Darius finished pummeling Kurt and then finished stripping him of his shorts, reaching down to fondle his bare ass. David turned away, closing his eyes, grimacing as he heard Kurt screaming out in pain as Darius made several harsh grunting sounds. Carver watched his brother raping the long-haired guy.

He never had much to say about Darius, but he did appreciate his brutality and willingness to follow orders.

Darius pounded himself into Kurt's ass, pulling his hair and slamming all of his thick pipe inside of the tight asshole. Kurt screamed in pain and the creeping sensation of pleasure, he never expected this in his life and now, he wished he had never tried to get away. He should have listened to David's plan, now, he had royally fucked both of them. In his case, quite literally.

The massive hillbilly continued to plow Kurt until he reached his natural conclusion and exploded inside of him, pulling out to drip the remaining drops on Kurt's bare ass, proud to see his handiwork. Kurt simply lay flat, the feeling of being violated filled his body and made him wea, the hillbilly had conquered him in the worst way. Darius raised up and turned to Carver, "I don't think he's gonna go nowhere."

"Seems that way to me," Carver smiled, looking down to David, "You want some, too?"

David opened his eyes, looking at the bearded man and shook his head, "No. I'll do as you say."

"Good," Carver replied, wringing out the water of the rag all over David's face and smiling, "Clean as a whistle."

The two heavy men raised their captives

up and brought them up the stairs, herding them like cows for the slaughter out of the cellar. Upon reaching the ground level of the house, David got a chance to look around and saw everything, not that it was much of a surprise to him.

The house was old. Probably two or three hundred years old and it looked as such. The living room featured ratty furniture, an old radio from the 50s that was playing static and next to it was an old man rocking back and forth. David spotted the hillbilly guy that had attacked them earlier, he was getting the knife wound on his back doctored by the cranky old lady, Mama. From the kitchen, he spotted another large mountain man looking over a stew that was filling up a huge dirty pot.

The overall feeling of the house was dirty.

Nothing about it looked clean to sit, sleep or eat in.

Hell, the cellar was cleaner than this place and it was hot, claustrophobic and had death everywhere in it. Mama Cannedy turned and saw the two, she frowned, "Carver! You and Darius put them at the table! We don't need them boys feeling comfortable in our house."

"Yes, mama," Carver replied, pushing the two into the dining room and forcing them in a pair of old wooden chairs, he then turned to them, "Y'all don't try nothing or I'll make sure your momma is on the menu!"

"We won't," David muttered, looking down at the table and seeing that it needed a really bad washing. Kurt whispered to David as the two brothers left, "I'm sorry."

"Forget it," David sighed, "Just follow my lead and don't try to run off again, these people ain't your typical hillbillies. They're smarter than I would have thought."

"Yeah," Kurt coughed, "I saw the one in the kitchen earlier today. He was talking to Carissa. I think she might have told him where we were going to be staying."

Of course, David groaned, leaving it to Carissa to get them in a trap. Fuck.

Felton Cannedy came into the kitchen to look at the guys and smiled at Kurt, "Oh, I remember you, Kurd or something, right?"

Kurt simply looked down at the table, unwilling to engage in the conversation or give the hillbilly the satisfaction of a response. It would be tantamount to surrender at this point in the game.

"Well, whatever your name is," Felton smiled smugly, "You should know your girlfriend got a good helping of me back at the cabin. She struggled a bit, but I can tell you that she is tighter than a trout's mouth and I know that from experience."

David looked up fiercely at Felton and growled, "Tell me you're lying."

"Nope," Felton chuckled, "I think I even got her virgin blood on my dick."

David started to rise from the chair until he realized he was still bound and stopped, shaking with anger. The man needed to die. All of them needed to die, but right now, the man talking to him was the one that deserved it most. David might not be his sister's biggest fan, but she did not deserve to be raped by an inbred hick, he was going to kill the motherfucker as soon as he could get up.

Mama Cannedy came in and looked at the guys, "Supper's ready. Felton, go get the girls and bring the woman, too. Best she gets some food before she meets the Lord with these two foul-mouthed fiends."

"Yes ma'am," Felton smiled at David and Kurt before departing for the stairs. David remained filled with anger and swearing an oath of vengeance in his mind. Kurt, meanwhile, silently cried as he hoped the man had been lying about Carissa.

But the truth could hurt much worse than a lie.

TEN

Carissa had been stripped of her clothing and fitted into a very tight garment made of animal-skin. Her hair was cut shorter.

Amethyst and Roon had told her their little scheme for escaping. It wasn't exactly sound-proof and she still wasn't sure she completely believed them, but she knew that anything would be better than whatever the family had in store for her.

The door to the room opened as Felton looked in and said, "Supper's on the table. Get y'alls asses down there."

"Okay," Roon spoke, pulling Carissa with Amethyst down the stairs and towards the dining room. David and Kurt both looked up to see Carissa sitting across from them. David looked at Roon and sneered, "You."

"Yes, me," Roon smiled, her eyes not

going along with the smile itself. Amethyst giggled, "He's cute."

Carissa shook her head, "Guys listen, we have serious fucking problem."

"Don't worry," David whispered, "I have a plan."

"So do we," Roon replied, earning a look of confusion from David. Kurt looked over to Carissa and sniffled, "Are you okay?"

"Yes," Carissa lied, seeing that he was visibly traumatized by something. Before she could speak further, the big men came in to sit a pot on the table and pass out small dirty bowls to everyone. The one who had been stabbed, Cleatus, came into the dining room carrying the old man and Mama followed behind, singing a hymn.

Mama Cannedy watched as everyone was seated, smiling a jagged toothed smile, "Bow your heads."

The men bowed, the old man simply stared into nothingness and everyone else kept looking at each other and the old lady. Mama Cannedy struck the table with her cane, "I. Said. Bow!"

David, Kurt, Carissa and the others bowed quickly; Mama smiling widely, speaking aloud a prayer filled with fire and brimstone that one would find in a backwoods church full of snake-handlers and poison-drinkers. Upon finishing with a group, "Amen," Cleatus started filling the bowls with the soup and passing it around to everyone.

Mama walked over to Carissa and caressed the side of her face, "You girls did a perdy good job with her. She looks like a pioneer woman now. You okay, dear?"

"No," Carissa snapped, "I'm far from okay. One of your inbred sons fucking raped me!"

"What?" Mama gasped, "Who?"

"The one who abducted me!"

Without missing a beat, Felton Cannedy returned with the body of Lenore and dropped her in a chair, turning to see everyone staring at him. He looked at them, "What?"

Mama quickly moved to him and slapped the towering man in the face,

"Damn you, boy! How dare you fornicate with that girl before marriage! Who gave you the right to make her yours out of wedlock!?"

Holding his face, Felton sighed, "I'm sorry, Mama, it was like love at first sight. I can't help it!"

Kurt looked at Carissa who simply sighed, not making eye contact with him as everyone else watched the scene unfold. Mama shook her head, "Well, now, I guess I can't fault ya for being in love. Since you done made her yours, I pronounce you two man and woman."

The hillbillies all clapped, except for the old man and the sisters. Carissa shook her head, standing out of her seat, "Fuck that! I'm not his woman! You people are fucking insane!"

Kurt spoke out, "She's already been spoken for!"

David closed his eyes, sighing heavily as the old lady and Felton turned to look at Kurt. Mama Cannedy narrowed her eyes at him, "By who? You?"

"Damn right," Carissa replied before being pulled back into the seat by Roon and Amethyst. Mama looked at Felton, "Well, my boy, it looks like you got someone that done claimed her first. You know how to settle that, so settle it."

Felton nodded, "With pleasure," walking over to Kurt and grabbed one of the knives from the table, using it to impale the man in his right eye, twisting the knife hard. Carissa screamed as David turned to see Kurt's face run red with blood from the knife in his eye socket. Kurt's body toppled out of the chair and onto the floor, blood pouring out around him as he lay still.

Felton turned to everyone, "It's settled," he said, turning to walk to his seat and start eating in silence. Mama turned to Carissa, "Don't you worry none, sweetheart, my boys are good men. They make the best lovers just like their daddy was. Papa and me were born almost seventy-four years to this day, twins in a family of fourteen. We had us a son together that was one of the nicest boys you could ever meet. My boy gave me these boys, sons and grandsons, no daughters though."

While Mama regaled her tale of vile family history, David reached under the table with his foot, pulling Kurt's head between his ankles. He then began moving his ankles up and down, using the bit of knife sticking out of Kurt's eye socket to cut through the leather strap, looking around to ensure nobody knew otherwise.

Mama continued, "So one day, after my son passed on and my grandsons were old enough, I said we need new blood. I ain't had no daughters, so we'd just get some and make them part of our home. Roon and Amethyst were our babies, found in that cabin you all were trespassing in, we brought them away to have a simple future with the rest of us. When they both turn sixteen next year, they're gonna be married off to Carver and Cleatus. Darius was supposed to be your man, but," she turned to Felton, "My youngest always has the best taste in everything. He told us all about you. How pretty you are. He was right, too."

Carissa pretended to listen to everything, looking down as tears filled her eyes, Kurt had been such a good man to her. She wished she had treated him better. She wished she'd fought harder back at the cabin. She had already lost her father and she could see her mom was slipping away, now she'd lost Kurt.

At this point, she began to think of ways to get killed by the family. Just let go and suffer in the afterlife, at least she would be with her family.

Mama finished her story, "Our family owns this mountain. Y'all come out here to fornicate and damage our lands, the deer don't even come up anymore because of all the intruders. So we make use of all y'all. Look at your bowl, sweetie, one of your friends and bits of your momma are gonna make your tummy full tonight. Oh, speaking of which, your momma don't seem to be very hungry."

Lenore's lay with her head on the table, staring into nothingness, having been tormented with cuts, scrapes, gropes and assault since she was brought to the house. Each of the men that had kidnapped her had taken a turn on her body and the old lady had ordered them to cut slices off of her flesh. The entire time she had only wanted to make sure that David and Carissa were safe. She needed to know her children were okay.

Yet, the family never told her, they simply continued to taunt, torment and mutilate her naked body.

She moved her eyes to see Carissa and tried to crack a smile, though the anguish of her existence was overwhelming her mind. It was a fucking tragedy, she thought to herself, everything she had tried to do had been for naught. She couldn't even help her kids now and she was right next to them, the bowl of food beside her face, the smell was foul.

Lenore prayed in her mind that her husband would come and save them, she couldn't understand why he wasn't here with them. She didn't know why he was gone. He should be there. He needed to be there. She needed him the most now.

She needed him to protect the kids as she felt herself starting to sink into a hole.

Mama looked at Cleatus and nodded, "Give the angel her wings."

Cleatus was up instantly and grabbed the back of Lenore's head, kicking the chair out from underneath her as he forced his massive knee into the back of her neck, giving a hard twist to her head. The sound of her spine shattering filled the air as Carissa screamed and David was hit with an instant mix of shock and anger, splitting his ankles apart as the leather broke.

He then ducked under the table, gripping the knife out of Kurt's eye and cut through the strap around his wrists. His arms and legs free, he sank the knife into the inner thigh of Darius, piercing through his artery, forcing blood to instantly flood through his pants.

Darius screamed out in agony as Mama and the others turned to see; the man stood up, blood shooting out of his leg wound as he attempted to get away from the table and David swung the knife again, cutting through his heel. Darius fell to the ground, "Mama! Help me!" he screamed as David slashed his throat instantly.

Cleatus looked under the table and grabbed David's leg, pulling him out from under it as David leaned up to send the knife directly into the man's crotch. Carissa watched with red and teary eyes, it was time to fight back.

ELEVEN

Cleatus fell back as blood squirted from the hole in his crotch, angrily yelling and crying out, "Kill him! Carver!"

Carver attempted to get out of his seat, but Carissa quickly reached over and grabbed the pot, dumping the hot soup all over him as he fell back in the chair, the force of the pot knocking him to the floor. She quickly got up and started stomping on him as best she could, only for Mama to grab her by her animal-skin outfit and pull her off of him.

Roon and Amethyst ran over to aid David, pulling Cleatus down as David leapt onto him, forcing the knife into his body at multiple places. The hulking man overpowered them, rising up to send a fist into David's face, knocking him across the table and onto Darius' blood-soaked corpse.

Carissa turned around and slapped Mama across the face, knocking the old lady into Papa. The two elders collided to the floor as the chair fell into one of the old oil lamps that was providing some light to the dimly-lit room. The flaming oil spread out onto the furniture, engulfing it into flame.

Carissa ran over to David, pulling him up, "Davy, get up! We gotta go!"

David looked around, dazed and jolted, but still alert to the situation. He started standing up, looking at Carissa, "I'm sorry."

Suddenly, a pickaxe flew directly between them and stuck into the wall, forcing them to jump back from each other. David turned to see Felton staring at them, a look of anger focused on Carissa as he reached down and overturned the table out of his way. He began making his way towards her as she moved into a corner.

Amethyst and Roon continued to do their best pummeling Cleatus as he slowly raised up off the floor. The two were too thin and petite to make much progress in beating him up, especially since their bodies were ruined from years of poor diet. The man knocked Roon to the floor with a fist to the face and grabbed Amethyst, she was Carver's bride-to-be, but she had clearly chosen to side against them.

Roon watched as Cleatus smashed Amethyst's face into the wall repeatedly until her head essentially busted all over the wall like a tick. Roon screamed and ran over to him, leaping on his back to bite into his ear, yanking her head around until it snapped off his head. Cleatus screamed in angry pain, grabbing at the bloody injury to the side of his head, he roared, "You little bitch!"

Meanwhile, Felton had Carissa pinned to the corner, considering what to do to her as the fighting and fire behind him had gotten out of hand.

David yanked the pickaxe out of the wall and raised it to swing into Felton. The hillbilly grabbed Carissa against him and turned to face David, having caught him out of the corner of his eye. He growled, "Kill me and you'll kill her too."

David held the pickaxe close, "Let her go!"

"Uh-uh," Felton motioned at him, "Drop that pick, boy. You done signed your death certificate. You ready to sign hers, too?"

David held the pickaxe, gripping it tightly and glared at Felton. He was right. If he tried to swing, the man would ensure that Carissa would get hit and then, he'd be taken down. He turned slightly, watching as Cleatus had Roon in a chokehold and was starting to squeeze the breath out of her.

Felton laughed, "What's it gonna be, boy?!"

David raised the pickaxe and quickly turned, throwing it directly into Cleatus. The pick stuck in him and he fell to the floor, dropping Roon in the process. Carissa took the chance and raised her bare foot up into Felton's crotch, forcing him to release her. She turned and shoved him right out of the window, knocking him into the coldness outside. She turned, breathing heavily as she ran towards David.

Suddenly, a shotgun blast caught everyone's attention as Mama held the weapon aimed at everyone, the fires had spread all over the living room and the house was filled with smoke. She looked at them, "Y'all done ruined supper and killed some of my boys! Vengeance is mine, sayeth the Lord, but I'm ready to bend the rule in this case!"

She aimed the shotgun.

Carver, on the floor, had come to and saw David holding Carissa in his arms. He growled, that little cunt had hit him and spilled the soup, it was time to teach them both a lesson. He raised up quickly to run into them.

Mama pulled the trigger and the buckshot instantly peppered Carver, tearing him into a cloud of bloody meat that splashed all over David and Carissa. Mama screamed, "No! I'm sorry, boy, oh Lord no!"

Roon, having recovered herself from the chokehold that Cleatus had forced onto her, quickly raised to her feet and leapt into Mama. Mama fell back as Roon dropped to the floor and within an instant, Mama was engulfed in the fiery hell that the living room had turned into. She screamed and angrily cursed everyone as her fiery figure ran all over the house, catching everything else aflame.

David grabbed Carissa's hand and headed out of the dining room, Carissa grabbing Roon as they headed for the front door. The upper level was starting to collapse into the ground floor and the fires were overwhelming the entire Cannedy house, the old wood bursting up in flames as the house collapsed.

Papa Cannedy stayed where he had fallen, unable to get up or leave, unable to speak. The flames surrounded him as he perished with the house itself and everyone else who had been killed, the entirety of the nightmare ending.

Outside, David, Carissa and Roon watched from the trail as the house was further engulfed in the flames and fires of death. Carissa hugged David, crying heavily as the traumatic events of the evening finally collapsed into her, both of them covered in blood and wounds. Roon looked at David and Carissa, "Thank you."

David simply stared at her until the girl simply nodded, turning away and headed off into the woods. He had nothing to say to her. They might have saved her and she might have helped them, but she was the reason for all of this. Had he not had Carissa to think about, David knew he would have strangled Roon to death right on the spot.

He showed mercy, letting her leave, but the thought of ever seeing her again made his blood run cold. David looked at his sister, "Come on, let's get back to the cabin and go get help."

The two made their way through a path that had been cleared through the cold dark forest. It was hard to see, despite the fires from the Cannedy house still burning brightly behind them, providing some illumination for their journey back to the cabin.

Walking in silence, Carissa wiped tears from her blood-caked face and felt the sting of losing Kurt and her mom over and over again. She had watched them both die and didn't try to help them, she should have tried. She should have tried to stop them.

They would have killed her, too.

At least then, she wouldn't have to live with the actions playing over and over again in her head, like a film reel from the deepest pits of hell itself. She was broken. The entire night had broken her worse than losing her father had. She knew David was hurting and she wanted to speak to him, but she couldn't think of the right words.

She didn't want to risk losing whatever peace they had between each other now.

The woods were dark, the cold winds coming off the mountain were swept with frigid pain against her bare legs and arms. The cold air and darkness reassured Carissa that she never wanted to see Mount Holcombe again for the rest of her life. It was something she would remember in her nightmares for years to come.

David's nightmares, too.

The pair finally made their way back to

the cabin, walking up on it as they saw the door open and darkness within. Exactly as it had been left, their mom's van was still sitting in front of the house. They walked inside and David flipped on the light switch, lighting up the cabin as both of them stopped to consider the situation.

Carissa looked at him, "You should shower first, just save me some hot water, yeah?"

"Okay," David nodded, turning to walk away from her towards the bathroom. She opened her mouth to speak to him, but nothing came out, she didn't know how to properly say any of it. It was too difficult and she wasn't ready to cry for hours, but she knew she would have to.

Sitting down at the table, she looked over the leftover food and rubbed her eyes, trying to make sense of the entire situation. They had come out for a family vacation and it turned into a nightmare, this was something that she had never expected.

The sound of footsteps filled her ears as she looked up to see if David was heading into the bathroom. She didn't see him. She simply sighed and rubbed her eyes more, until an horrifyingly familiar voice spoke to her, "Howdy, darlin', I never did get your name."

She turned over her shoulder and her face twisted in fright, she screamed.

Felton Cannedy stood in the doorway, his hulking body towered over her and his hands held a pickaxe tightly.

About the Author

Bestselling Author of Trash Horror!

Jerry Blaze is an award-nominated author of

extreme splatterpunk fiction

After achieving success in the erotic market, Jerry decided to undertake extreme horror/splatterpunk and found some acclaim.

Jerry is a fan of grindhouse and exploitation films from the 70s and 80s, often modeling his work on them. He currently lives in the American Midwest, but travels often to get inspiration or to run away from angry mobs.

Media Links:

Facebook: Jerry Blaze

TikTok: @Jblazehorror

Instagram: OfficialJerryBlaze

Website: jblazehorror.com

Gmail: jblazehorror@gmail.com

Printed in Dunstable, United Kingdom